D0010353

JANE DYER

Little Brown Bear and the Bundle of Joy

LITTLE, BROWN AND COMPANY

New York ❧ Boston

Also by Jane Dyer

Little Brown Bear Won't Take a Nap!
Little Brown Bear Won't Go to School!
Animal Crackers

Copyright © 2005 by Jane Dyer

All rights reserved. No part of this book may be reproduced in any form or by any electronic or mechanical means, including information storage and retrieval systems, without permission in writing from the publisher, except by a reviewer who may quote brief passages in a review.

Little, Brown and Company

Time Warner Book Group
1271 Avenue of the Americas, New York, NY, 10020
Visit our Web site at www.lb-kids.com

First Edition

Library of Congress Cataloging-in-Publication Data

Dyer, Jane.
  Little Brown Bear and the bundle of joy / Jane Dyer. — 1st ed.
    p. cm.
  Summary: When Little Brown Bear learns that his parents are expecting "a bundle of
joy," he sets out to discover what that means and is not at all happy with what he learns.
  ISBN 0-316-17469-6
  [1. Babies — Fiction. 2. Bears — Fiction. 3. Parent and child — Fiction. 4. Brothers and
sisters—Fiction. 5. Animals—Fiction.] I. Title.

PZ7.D977Le 2004
[E] — dc22

                                                                        2003052092

10 9 8 7 6 5 4 3 2 1

SC

Manufactured in China

The illustrations for this book were done in Holbein watercolor
on Waterford 140-lb. hot-press paper.

The text was set in Usherwood, and the display type is P22 Garamouche.

For Maria, again

Mama and Papa Bear were very busy.

"What's going on?" asked Little Brown Bear.

"We're getting ready for our little bundle of joy," answered Mama.

"What's a bundle of joy?" Little Brown Bear asked.

Papa said, "You'll find out soon enough!"

"I want to know right now!" declared Little Brown Bear. "What is a little bundle of joy?"

But Mama Bear and Papa Bear were so busy they didn't hear him.

Little Brown Bear decided to go ask Owl. *She is very wise,* he thought to himself. *She will know the answer.*

As he walked along, Little Brown Bear wondered, *Could a bundle of joy be a bundle of toys? Or maybe honey cakes?*

"Whooo's there?" called Owl from high up in her tree.

"It's Little Brown Bear. I've come to ask you a question. What's a little bundle of joy?"

Owl smiled. "Why, I have a little bundle of joy right here."

She invited him to climb up and see.

Little Brown Bear peeked into Owl's nest. There lay an owlet, who immediately began screeching.

"*That's* a little bundle of joy?" he asked in disbelief.

The noise was too loud for Little Brown Bear. He scrambled back down the tree as fast as he could.

Little Brown Bear ran and ran until he came upon a farm.

"Whoa!" called Horse. "What's the matter?"

"My parents are getting a little bundle of joy, but I don't want one. They're too loud."

"Not *my* bundle of joy!" replied Horse.

"You have a little bundle of joy, too?" Little Brown Bear asked.

Horse told him to be very quiet and follow her.

Little Brown Bear tiptoed behind Horse until they came upon a sleeping foal.

Horse whispered, "Isn't she precious?"

Little Brown Bear thought that the foal was rather boring, but he thanked Horse and quietly slipped away.

Next, Little Brown Bear came to the barnyard. There, he saw Pig, who asked how he was.

Little Brown Bear explained, "My parents are getting ready for a little bundle of joy and I don't want one. They're boring!"

"Hogwash!" squealed Pig. "Come see *my* little bundles of joy. They are not the least bit boring."

Little Brown Bear saw five perky piglets playing in the mud. They were certainly not boring, but they were quite messy (not to mention stinky).

So off he went.

Little Brown Bear sat down to think. *How could Mama and Papa want such a bundle of joy? They don't like it when* I'm *messy.*
Just then, Frog noticed him. "What's wrong?" she asked.

Little Brown Bear told Frog about his problem.
Frog smiled as she pointed to her tadpoles and explained,
"Babies aren't always noisy or boring or messy."

"BABIES?" questioned Little Brown Bear. "Who said anything about babies?"

"Your mama and papa are going to have a baby," reassured Frog.
"That's what 'little bundle of joy' means."

Little Brown Bear looked confused.

Frog thought for a minute and then said, "Come with me."

Frog led Little Brown Bear to the park. Babies were everywhere. Some babies were crying, some were sleeping, and some were making mud pies.

Families were all around. Little Brown Bear noticed that many babies had big brothers and sisters playing with them. It looked like fun.

Little Brown Bear decided he had better get home to *his* family.

When Little Brown Bear arrived at his house, he could hear the cry of a newborn baby.

Mama and Papa were very happy to see him.

"Here is your new baby sister!" they announced proudly.

The baby stopped crying when she saw Little Brown Bear. She looked up at him and smiled.

"Is she your little bundle of joy?" asked Little Brown Bear.

"Yes, she is," answered Mama and Papa Bear, "but you are our BIG bundle of joy!"

J PICTURE DYER
Dyer, Jane.
Little Brown Bear and
 the bundle of joy /

EAST ATLANTA

Atlanta-Fulton Public Library